EARLY BIRD STORIES™

My Family Celebrates
DAY OF THE DEAD

Lisa Bullard

Illustrated by Holli Conger

LERNER PUBLICATIONS ◆ MINNEAPOLIS

NOTE TO EDUCATORS

Find text recall questions at the end of each chapter. Critical-thinking and text feature questions are available on page 23. These help young readers learn to think critically about the topic by using the text, text features, and illustrations.

Lerner Publications Company
A division of Lerner Publishing Group, Inc.
241 First Avenue North
Minneapolis, MN 55401 USA

For reading levels and more information, look up this title at www.lernerbooks.com.

Photos on page 22 used with permission of: Shandor/Shutterstock.com (candy skulls); Champ-Ritthikrai/Shutterstock.com (marigolds); DUQUE/Shutterstock.com (La Catrina skeletons).

Main body text set in Billy Infant 22/28.
Typeface provided by SparkyType.

Library of Congress Cataloging-in-Publication Data

Names: Bullard, Lisa, author. | Conger, Holli, illustrator.
Title: My family celebrates Day of the Dead / Lisa Bullard ; illustrated by Holli Conger.
Description: Minneapolis : Lerner Publications, 2019. | Series: Holiday time (early bird stories) | Includes bibliographical references and index. | Audience: Age 5-8. | Audience: K to Grade 3.
Identifiers: LCCN 2018006007 (print) | LCCN 2017049347 (ebook) | ISBN 9781541524972 (eb pdf) | ISBN 9781541520080 (lb : alk. paper) | ISBN 9781541527393 (pb : alk. paper)
Subjects: LCSH: All Souls' Day—Juvenile literature. | Mexico—Social life and customs—Juvenile literature.
Classification: LCC GT4995.A4 (print) | LCC GT4995.A4 B793 2019 (ebook) | DDC 394.266—dc23

LC record available at https://lccn.loc.gov/2018006007

Manufactured in the United States of America
1-44344-34590-1/12/2018

TABLE OF CONTENTS

CHAPTER 1

WAITING FOR DAY OF THE DEAD

Hi! I'm Daniela, and I can't wait for Day of the Dead! It was my grandpa's favorite holiday.

It's an important holiday in Mexico. But some families in the United States celebrate it too.

On Day of the Dead, we remember people who have died. My school friends think it sounds sad.

But Grandpa always said it is a happy time.

Why does Daniela celebrate Day of the Dead?

CHAPTER 2

AN ALTAR FOR GRANDPA

This year, I'm remembering Grandpa. He died a few months ago.

Mama says Grandpa will be back to visit us on Day of the Dead! I won't see him, but I'll know he's here.

We make our *ofrenda*, or altar. It's for Grandpa and other loved ones who have died.

That's where we put Day of the Dead things, like Grandpa's picture and his favorite hat.

What did Daniela make for her grandpa?

11

AT THE MARKET

Mama and I pick out sugar skulls at the market. We also buy funny little skeletons.

We buy bread of the dead from the baker.

Yum! I'll be sure to leave lots for Grandpa on the altar.

Where did Daniela buy sugar skulls?

CELEBRATING!

On Day of the Dead, we visit the cemetery. We clean Grandpa's grave.

We leave marigolds for him to smell.

17

Lots of family members come to visit later. Everyone tells funny stories, especially about Grandpa.

I laugh until my belly aches. Or maybe that's because I ate too many tamales!

Day of the Dead is almost over. I'm going to keep Grandpa's hat in my room.

LEARN ABOUT HOLIDAYS

Day of the Dead is an important holiday in Mexico and other parts of Central and South America. Some families in the United States also celebrate it.

The Aztecs once lived in part of Mexico. They believed the dead visited during a special time every year. The Spanish came to Mexico in 1519. The Spanish were Christians. They remembered people who died on November 1 and 2. Day of the Dead combines these Aztec and Christian ideas.

Skeletons and sugar skulls are common Day of the Dead decorations. They remind people of death but are not meant to be scary.

Families visiting graves of their loved ones bring marigolds. The Aztecs connected these flowers with death.

Aztecs ate tamales long ago. Many people think of them as celebration food. They are made from corn dough, filled with meat or vegetables, and cooked inside corn husks or leaves.

THINK ABOUT HOLIDAYS:
CRITICAL-THINKING AND TEXT FEATURE QUESTIONS

Why do some families celebrate Day of the Dead?

How is Day of the Dead different from other holidays? How is it the same?

What did the table of contents tell you about this book?

What are the names of the chapters in this book?

GLOSSARY

altar: a table or space to place religious items or, during Day of the Dead, items for and about dead people who are being remembered

cemetery: an area where dead bodies are buried

grave: the specific spot where a dead body is buried

ofrenda: the Spanish word for *offering* and what Spanish-speaking people call a Day of the Dead altar

skeleton: the bones that support a human or animal body

TO LEARN MORE

BOOKS

Barner, Bob. *The Day of the Dead/El Dia De Los Muertos.* New York: Holiday House, 2010. Learn all about the festivities of Day of the Dead in this picture book in English and Spanish.

Thong, Roseanne Greenfield. *Dia de Los Muertos.* Chicago: Albert Whitman, 2015. In this book, join the children getting ready to celebrate Day of the Dead as they decorate and prepare altars.

WEBSITE

National Geographic Kids: **Day of the Dead**
http://kids.nationalgeographic.com/explore/celebrations/day-of-the-dead/
Day of the Dead traditions come to life through bright photos.

INDEX

24